Put Beginning Readers on the Right Track with ALL ABOARD READING™

The All Aboard Reading series is especially for beginning readers. Written by noted authors and illustrated in full color, these are books that children really and truly *want* to read—books to excite their imagination, tickle their funny bone, expand their interests, and support their feelings. With four different reading levels, All Aboard Reading lets you choose which books are most appropriate for your children and their growing abilities.

Picture Readers—for Ages 3 to 6
Picture Readers have super-simple texts, with many nouns appearing as rebus pictures. At the end of each book are 24 flash cards—on one side is the rebus picture; on the other side is the written-out word.

Level 1—for Preschool through First-Grade Children
Level books have very few lines per page, very large type, easy words, lots of repetition, and pictures with visual "cues" to help children figure out the words on the page.

Level 2—for First-Grade to Third-Grade Children
Level 2 books are printed in slightly smaller type than Level 1 books. The stories are more complex, but there is still lots of repetition in the text, and many pictures. The sentences are quite simple and are broken up into short lines to make reading easier.

Level 3—for Second-Grade through Third-Grade Children
Level 3 books have considerably longer texts, harder words, and more complicated sentences.

All Aboard for happy reading!

To Carol and Patricia:
This one's for you—S.A.K.

Photo credits: front cover, Nathaniel Butler / Allsport; back cover, Elsa Hasch / Allsport; title page, Paul Bereswill / Sports Illustrated; p. 7, Jim McIsaac / Bruce Bennett Studios; p. 11, Rick Stewart / Allsport; p. 18, Bruce Bennett Studios; p. 20, Lane Stewart / Sports Illustrated; p. 24, Jerry Wachter / Sports Illustrated; p. 27, Paul Bereswill / Sports Illustrated; p. 34, Paul Bereswill / Sports Illustrated; p. 40, David E. Klutho / Sports Illustrated; p. 43, Gregory Heisler / Sports Illustrated; p. 47, Ian Tomlinson / Allsport; p. 48, Gregory Heisler / Sports Illustrated.

Library of Congress Cataloging-in-Publication Data is available.

ISBN 0-448-42157-7 (GB)   A B C D E F G H I J
ISBN 0-448-42156-9 (pbk.)   A B C D E F G H I J

ALL
ABOARD
READING™
Level 3
Grades 2-3

THE GREAT GRETZKY

By S.A. Kramer
Illustrated by Ken Call
With photographs

Grosset & Dunlap • New York

The Last Game

April 18, 1999. It's a quiet Sunday afternoon in New York City. But at Madison Square Garden, a sellout crowd is making a lot of noise. The New York Rangers are about to play the Pittsburgh Penguins. Some people have paid a thousand dollars a ticket to watch. Yet no one in the arena seems to want the game to start. Instead, 18,200 fans call out one athlete's name over and over—Wayne Gretzky. Wayne is about to play his last NHL game ever.

The stands are filled with people wearing his jersey and his number, 99.

Others wave signs saying "Thank You, Wayne," "No Regretzkys," and "99 Forever." When Wayne finally skates into the rink, they go wild.

Dressed in Ranger red, white, and blue, Wayne smiles at the crowd. On center ice, old teammates and a coach surround him and give him hugs. The National Hockey League commissioner announces that the number 99 will be retired. That means no player can ever wear it again. For fifteen solid minutes, the fans stand and cheer.

It's hard for them to believe Wayne is leaving hockey. Thirty-eight years old, he's played in 1,487 games. But now he feels tired. This past season, he's been hurt. The Rangers have begged him to stay. But Wayne says, "My gut and my heart are telling me this is the right time."

Just two days ago, he told reporters his decision. Since then, the President of the United States has called him, and the Canadian Prime Minister made a speech

about him. Yesterday his teammates gave him a special gift—a leather chair in the shape of a baseball glove, since Wayne has loved baseball all his life. Fans have sent him presents, too.

But why is everyone making such a fuss? What's the big deal about a hockey player's last game?

Wayne is the best player in NHL history. Even more important, he and his

hockey style changed the game forever. His nickname says it all—The Great One.

Wayne was a pale, skinny guy in a sport of big, powerful men. While most of them shoved, checked, and fought, Wayne scored—and scored again—without using violence. In the rink all around him were quicker, stronger players. But Wayne understood the game better than they did and just couldn't be stopped. In twenty seasons, he won ten scoring titles, four Stanley Cups, and nine Most Valuable Player awards. He became hockey's scoring leader, showing fans you don't have to be rough to be tops.

Wayne did more for hockey than just play the game well. Before he came along, it was a small-time sport in America. His skill and popularity made it big time.

Leaving hockey isn't easy for Wayne. Right now, his emotions are running high. As he gets ready to play, his hands are shaking so much, he has trouble lacing his skates up. But he knows his family is behind him. They're at the arena to see him off—his mom and dad, and his wife and three kids.

At last the action begins, and it's just like old times. There's Wayne racing past the blue line and passing for an assist. Each time he gets the puck, fans scream with excitement. He may be retiring, but he still has the magic touch.

The Rangers lose 2–1 in overtime. It's a shame Wayne's last game isn't a win.

Still, the crowd rises to its feet cheering. Wayne turns and starts his good-byes.

Ever the gentleman, he shakes hands with each opponent. His blue eyes filled with tears, he hugs every one of his teammates. Then he skates around the rink, waving to fans and blowing kisses to his wife. All the while, both Rangers and Penguins bang their sticks on the ice. That's the hockey way to pay tribute to a player.

The fans don't want to let Wayne go. They throw flowers into the rink, along with hats, jackets, shoes, even a wallet. His teammates don't want him to leave either. For one lap they follow him around the ice, clapping for him the whole way.

Suddenly the arena goes black. A single spotlight shines down on Wayne. In the darkness, he skates one last lap, all alone.

Right now, he might be remembering how he learned the game as a toddler. Or the trouble he had as a teenager finding a team that would accept him. He might be thinking about all the experts who said he was too wimpy for the NHL.

How did a nice guy like Wayne become the king of hockey?

The Little Hotshot

It was in November, 1963, that Wayne put on his first pair of skates. Just two years old, he glided smoothly down a frozen river by his grandparents' farm. His father was there with his camera to catch it on film.

But it was probably his grandmother who first noticed his talent. Sitting in her chair, she watched little Wayne slide across the wooden floor as though it were ice. With his child's hockey stick, the two-year-old would try to slap a rubber ball between her feet. Grandma goalie blocked some shots, but quite a few went through.

By the time Wayne was four, it was clear that he was a natural athlete. He loved to play hockey in the outdoor rink in the local park. His parents felt that with practice, he would master the game.

There was just one problem. The Gretzkys lived in the town of Brantford in Ontario, Canada. Brantford winters are cold, with temperatures often near zero. That didn't bother Wayne—skating kept him warm. But his dad froze while he stood around to keep an eye on his son.

So Mr. Gretzky came up with a plan.
He left the garden sprinkler on one night
and flooded the backyard. The wintry
weather froze the water into Wayne's own
private rink. Now the boy could practice
for hours, while his father sat inside in the
warmth and watched.

By the time Wayne was six, he could outplay everyone his age. He was so much better than they were, he was allowed to join the ten-year-olds' team. People were amazed that skinny little Wayne could hold his own against boys twice his size. Soon he was the youngest All-Star on his local team.

Wayne loved hockey so much that practicing was fun. Every day before and after school, he'd practice for hours in the backyard. At dinner he'd eat quickly, with his skates still on. Then he'd practice until bedtime.

Wayne's skill on the ice made him the talk of Ontario. Nobody had ever seen a young boy score so easily. By the time he was nine, reporters were coming to watch him play. A writer nicknamed him The Great One, and it stuck.

Hockey wasn't the only sport Wayne was good at. He played golf, lacrosse, and ran track. In the summer, he pitched for a local baseball team. He had so much talent, he once struck out nineteen batters.

Years later he confessed, "My dream was
to pitch for the Detroit Tigers."

Come fall, though, Wayne was back in
the rink. Hockey was always his first love.
He believed that one day he might be an
NHL star. That's why in class sometimes,
he'd practice his autograph.

It was a good thing he did. By the time
he was ten, people were asking him for it.
That's because he scored 378 goals in just
69 games, including three in 45 seconds!

He was on a TV special. There was even a hockey card issued for him.

Wayne was famous throughout Canada! Adult fans began to crowd the rinks to see him play. After games, people pushed and shoved so hard to reach him, sometimes he needed a police escort.

Fame didn't come without a price. Wayne was a shy kid. Being in the spotlight made him blush. With big crowds watching his every move, playing wasn't pure fun anymore. If he had a bad game, people complained.

There was worse. The parents of some of his teammates got angry at him. After all, Wayne was so good, he got all the attention. The other kids on the team never got credit for a win. A few parents actually started to boo him when he took the ice. By the time he was fourteen, his hometown junior hockey team refused to give him a spot. It looked like he might have to stop playing.

Then a team for older players in the big city of Toronto invited him to join. But to do that, he'd have to leave home and live with another family. Some of his opponents would be twenty years old.

Wayne's parents objected. They were afraid the older players might injure their teenage son. Besides, they wanted Wayne home with them, not away in a strange city. But the boy was desperate to play and convinced them to let him go.

Wayne was lonely in Toronto. He called his family every night. Still, he knew he'd done the right thing. He was the runt of his team, but his size didn't matter. Averaging nearly three points a game, he was junior hockey's boy wonder. By the age of sixteen, he'd signed his first pro contract. *Sports Illustrated* ran a story about him.

At eighteen, Wayne was in the NHL. To him it was a dream come true. All that hometown booing seemed far behind him. But he knew the real test of his talent was only beginning. Now he'd find out how good he really was.

Superstar

October 10, 1979, Wayne's first NHL game. Only a rookie, he was set to play center for the Edmonton Oilers. Before taking the ice, he was a bundle of nerves. His parents were worried—he had a fever and a terrible sore throat.

But something else was bothering Wayne. Though he had yet to skate a step in the NHL, reporters were calling him a flop. One wrote that Wayne was "as phony as a three-dollar bill." Experts said he was too small and slow for the NHL, that he'd be crushed against the boards by the league's speeding giants.

The critics made Wayne mad. But he didn't show his feelings. He knew there was only one way to prove himself—get out on the ice and score.

In his first NHL game, he had an assist. He didn't get a goal until his third game—but then there was no stopping him.

By season's end, his critics were quiet. They had to be. Wayne was the youngest player ever to have fifty goals in one year. He was also the only rookie in NHL history to be named Most Valuable Player. But perhaps his biggest accomplishment was just staying on his skates. His season-long sore throat turned out to be a pretty serious sickness—tonsillitis!

In the next few years, fans poured into arenas to see Wayne play. They cheered both his goals and the way he scored them. Wayne was a model of sportsmanship. Rival teams tried to get him to fight, but he kept his focus. While other men skated like they were playing bumper cars, Wayne just got the puck in the net.

He was easy to spot anywhere in the rink. At 5'11", 170 pounds, he was often the shortest, thinnest guy in skates. His jersey was too big and tucked in on the

right side. He'd worn it like that since childhood, when he had to keep his stick from catching in his shirt. Now he was so convinced he wouldn't score if the jersey came loose that he velcroed it to his pants!

Skating bent over at the waist, left-handed Wayne invented new hockey moves. He would charge over the blue line

toward the boards, only to stop suddenly and spin around. Controlling the puck with his great stickhandling, he let other players race by. Then he'd slam a quick pass to a teammate, who'd go in for a score.

Unlike other centers, Wayne would take the puck behind the other team's net. He skated there so often, it was called his

"office." Seeing at a glance where each player was, he'd pass for an assist at just the right moment, or he'd flick in a wraparound goal himself.

In his office, he was unstoppable. Even when he seemed trapped, he found a way to score. In a 1981 game, he was surrounded by St. Louis Blues. There was nowhere to go. So he flipped the puck over the cage onto the goalie's back. It bounced off the man—and into the net!

That wasn't the first time Wayne hit the puck off another object into the cage. Like no skater before him, he played all the shooting angles. He'd score by banging the puck off the boards right between the posts. He'd smash it off someone else's stick. In one playoff game, he slapped it off a defenseman's skate. It went into the net for the winning goal!

Whenever his line was on the ice, Wayne controlled the game. As though he had radar, he knew where the puck was every instant. Sometimes he guessed where an opponent would go even before the man moved. Most players looked at the ice and saw a blur of sticks, skates, and bodies. Not Wayne. He said, "To me, it's like everything's happening in slow motion."

It didn't matter that he had a weak slapshot and couldn't shoot well from a distance. Wayne had great balance, a quick first step, and slippery moves. While bodies fell all around him as players were hooked, high-sticked, and tripped, no

one touched Wayne. Checking him, one reporter said, was "like stopping a puff of smoke."

He was a scoring machine. Close to the net, he practically never missed. He could get a goal anywhere, anytime, even on face-offs. In one game, he got two goals in nine seconds. The opposing coach was desperate—he had to stop Wayne. So he pulled the first goalie and sent in a second.

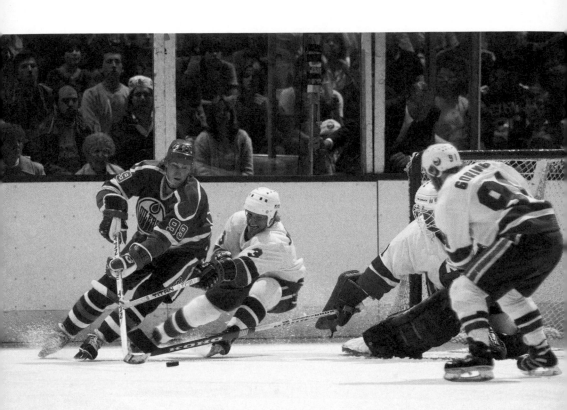

Wayne didn't mind. He scored twice again. That gave him four goals in one period against two different men.

Fans and experts alike were amazed by his scoring feats. In just his third year in the NHL, Wayne became the only player ever to get 200 points in a single season. He also had 92 goals—a record that may never be broken. In 1983–84, he got at least one point in fifty-one games in a row. Now he was famous worldwide.

Wayne seemed to have it all. But there was one thing missing—the Stanley Cup. To him, winning the Cup was the truest sign of an athlete's greatness. He felt his records and trophies would mean nothing without a championship.

Yet some experts believed he would never win one. Wayne had the talent, they said, but not the grit. After all, he and the Oilers seemed to lose whenever it really counted. They'd been to the playoffs four times already, and only reached the finals once. Then they had been swept. Wayne hadn't even scored. Reporters wrote that Wayne choked under Cup pressure.

Would he be able to prove his critics wrong again?

The Great One

May, 1984, Edmonton, Canada. It was the fourth game of the Stanley Cup finals. The Oilers had a 2–1 lead in the series against the New York Islanders. But as critics predicted, Wayne hadn't been much help to his team. So far the Islanders had stopped him cold.

Wayne was miserable. The Islanders had a special way of guarding him that he couldn't get around. They kept a man on him even after he'd passed off the puck. That way Wayne's teammates couldn't get it back to him for a goal.

But just the day before Wayne had come up with an idea. He wouldn't pass until he was clear of the man. Then with open ice in front of him, he'd take a return pass and score.

In the very first period, he shook off the defenseman. The new move was working! Wayne broke free down the middle. Getting a pass from a teammate, he raced right at the goalie. Then he faked one way and shot the other. Score!

 The huge crowd in the arena jumped up and cheered. Wayne's slump was over. Now the Oilers were on their way. Wayne wrote later, "That felt like the biggest goal of my career."

 Wayne scored again that night as the Oilers went on to win. Then in the next game he had another two goals—and a championship at last.

As fans poured onto the ice, he began to cry. His little brother burst into the rink, leaping into his arms. With balloons and streamers filling the air, Wayne put him on his shoulders and skated a victory lap. Then he grabbed hold of the Stanley Cup and held it high.

As the seasons passed, Wayne skated with even more confidence. In 1985–86, he scored the most points ever in one year—215. With Wayne as captain, the Oilers won another three Stanley Cups. He was honored again and again.

But Wayne was a superstar with a difference. Most scoring leaders always wanted the puck. Not Wayne. As long as a goal was scored, he didn't care who got it. Totally unselfish, he'd set up a play and pass off. He was the game's best passer,

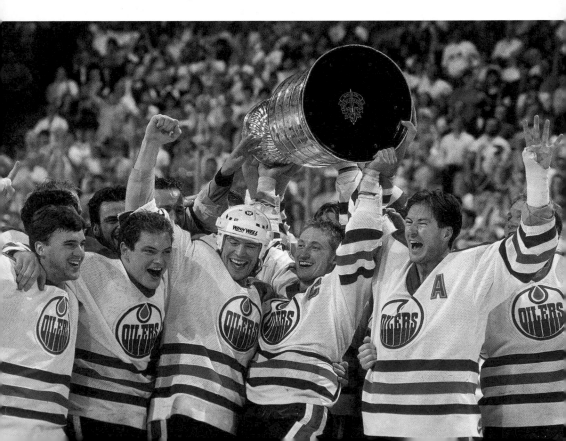

always putting the team first. No one had ever played hockey quite this way before.

If there was an open man on the ice, Wayne always found him. His no-look passes stunned both athletes and fans. Sometimes he didn't even need a stick to get the puck to a teammate. Without missing a step, he used his foot! No wonder that in 1985–86, he had a record 163 assists.

Wayne was the complete team player. Still, he had his own way of doing things. When he dressed for a game, he always put his equipment and uniform on the same way, in the same order. Though his teammates lifted weights, Wayne refused. When the Oilers were tested for strength, he came in last!

While he didn't care about muscles, he was fussy about his equipment. He used short, heavy sticks that had to be exactly the same weight. If one was a quarter of an ounce off, he wouldn't touch it.

His skates had to be just right, too. To support his weak ankles, he wore his skates too small. Then he would curl his double-jointed toes up inside.

But away from the ice, Wayne was an easygoing guy. While some athletes use their fame to get special treatment, Wayne

said, "I don't consider myself bigger or
better than anyone."

Ever polite, he always gave interviews
to reporters. Whenever a fan wanted an
autograph, he'd sign. He made friends
with workers in the clubhouse, from the
security guards to the boys who carried
in the towels. He took rookies under his
wing. With his kindness and even temper,
Wayne was a role model for fans.

In Canada, he had made hockey more
popular than ever. Then in 1988, he got

the chance to do the same in the U.S. That's when he was traded to the Los Angeles Kings.

Before Wayne, there were few hockey fans in warm-weather places. But with a hockey hero in L.A., people started filling the Kings' arena. Cities like Miami and Dallas demanded teams, too.

Thanks to Wayne, hockey became one of America's favorite sports. That's why even movie stars and a mayor turned out to watch him break hockey's most important record. It was March 23, 1994, and Wayne had a chance to become the all-time leader in goals.

It happened on a power play in the

second period against the Vancouver Canucks. As Wayne skated near the crease, a teammate passed him the puck. While it was still in the air, Wayne swung and connected. The puck slammed into the cage. Goal!

"I did it!" a thrilled Wayne shouted. He had made Number 802.

There were more scores to come, and for different teams. Late in the 1995–96 season, Wayne joined the St. Louis Blues. The next year he took the ice for the Rangers.

He was getting older, but he was still one of the best. In 1997–98, his next-to-last year, he led the league in assists. He got two hat tricks in playoff games. His last season, he was named the All-Star game MVP.

By the time Wayne retired, he held

He's gone from the sport now, but no one will forget Wayne Gretzky. In a game that prizes violence, he was a gentleman of the rink. Though he wasn't tall, tough, or fast, he outskated and outthought everyone. He is truly The Great One.

sixty-one NHL records. He has the most
goals (894), the most assists (1,963), and
the most points (2,857) ever. An eighteen-
time All-Star, he also won the trophy for
sportmanship four times. To cap it all off,
he was voted into the Hall of Fame early.